JUST JUNIPER

The First Adventure

D1507159

Go on more adventures with JUNIPER!

JUST JUNIPER-The First Adventure (Book 1)

The Mystery of the Mountain Lion Tracks(Book 2)

The Secret at the Lighthouse (Book 3)

Dolphins to the Rescue (Book 4)

Twin Trouble at Turtle Top (Book 5)

Coming soon...

The Disappearing Snowman (Book 6)

Dog Day at The Deering Estate (Book 7)

Barney's Big Surprise

JUST JUNIPER

The First Adventure

Written by Irene Hernández

Illustrated by Silvia María de la Fé

Book 1 of *JUST JUNIPER Series*

JUST JUNIPER Adventures

JustJuniperAdventures.com

The Library of Congress
Registration Number **TXu 2-136-279**
February 16, 2019
JUST JUNIPER Adventures- chapter book serie

JUST JUNIPER
The First Adventure

This book is dedicated to my second-grade students whose enthusiasm for the real Juniper inspired me to write the books...and of course to Juniper!

I also want to thank Elein, Emily, Kristina and my sister Lulú for all their help. I can't forget to thank my nephew Joey who played classical music to inspire his mother to draw all the illustrations and covers for the JUST JUNIPER Series.

CONTENTS

Chapter 1 – The Discovery

I sat up on my bed. The sound of a dog barking woke me up.

Is that Juniper?

No, it can't be Juniper, she never barks, I said to myself.

I covered my head with my pillow and tried to go back to sleep. The barking started again. This time louder. "Woof!" "Woof!"

It sounded like Juniper!

I jumped out of bed and ran down the stairs. Juniper was standing with her paws on the windowsill looking out of the dining room window and barking.

I ran over to her, wrapped my arms around her and tried to calm her. "Juni, what is it?" She stopped barking for a second and looked at me. I looked out the window. It was still dark outside. Juniper started barking again and started pulling me towards the front door.

"Juniper, it is dark outside. Stop barking, you are going to wake up Dad!"

Juniper stopped barking and looked at me as if she understood, but she did not stop yanking at my pajamas.

Juniper is my dog, a two-year-old Golden Retriever and she is very big and strong. Juni is very sweet but she can be really stubborn when she wants something. She would not stop pulling me. I was holding her by the collar, but she kept dragging me towards the door.

"Juni, stop!" I repeated.

She stopped pulling for a second and looked at the door. She started barking again. "Sophie, what's going on?" my Dad asked from his bedroom. "Is something wrong?"

"No Dad, don't worry, everything is OK," I said, "it's just Juniper!"

"Get her to stop barking right now! It's 5 in the morning!"

"Juniper, please be quiet" I pleaded. Juniper stopped barking but ran to the front door.

"OK, OK!" I said "I'll take you outside".

I was scared to go out when it was still dark because my Dad's house in North Carolina is on a mountain top. Sometimes there are wild animals roaming around at night.

Juniper had never done this before, she is a sleepy head. I am always the one who has to wake her up in the morning.

"Juni, I am going to go outside with you but please don't go far."

I decided to put her on her leash to keep her close to me.

"It is not safe to be outside at this time, there could be a bobcat out there" I told her. I knew she understood me by the serious look on her face but she kept pulling on her leash. I opened the door, Juniper ran out so fast that she almost made me fall.

"Juniper, slow down," I whispered.

I did not want my Dad to know we were going outside. We were never supposed to be outside the house by ourselves when it was dark.

There was no slowing Juniper down.

She dragged me to the side of the house by the garage and started whimpering. She stopped next to the rose bushes, she looked at me and kept whimpering.

"Juniper, what do you want?" I asked her, "I am freezing out here."

It was cold outside and I was barefoot and shivering, the wind was blowing hard and my black curly hair was all tangled and covering my eyes so I could hardly see.

Juniper would not move. She just stood there looking at the rose bush and whimpering.

Suddenly I realized that the whimpering was not coming from just Juniper.

I heard another sound. I looked around trying to find where it was coming from. There was a cardboard box under the rose bush.

The sound was coming from the box!

Chapter 2 – The Box

I stood staring at the box. Juniper was
looking at the box also. We were frozen,
unable to move, just staring in disbelief.
The box started to shake, and the sound
got louder. It was a puppy's whimper!

Juniper seemed to be saying, "You see, I was right! We had to come outside even if it was dark and cold!"

She was right, we had to come outside. I'm glad she convinced me.

When I opened the box all I could see was a bundle wrapped in a blue flannel shirt. I knew it was a puppy, but I was too nervous to uncover it.

I took a very deep breath and got the courage to pick it up.

The puppy's body felt warm in my arms, quiet and relaxed.

I was so nervous I did not even dare to look at it.

How long has the puppy been in that box? Who left it here? Why?

There is no way my Dad can find out about this puppy. He was mad enough when I got Juniper. He loves Juniper a lot now, but it was an ordeal at first.

"Juni, what are we going to do with this puppy?" I asked her. "You know we can't tell Dad!"

Juniper's face told me she knew exactly what I was saying. I'm glad Juni knows that my Dad really loves her now. It took a while but now he adores Juniper.

That is how my Dad is.

The puppy was still completely wrapped in the flannel shirt. The warm body was relaxed and keeping me warm.

It was cold outside, but I had not moved because I could tell that the puppy had fallen asleep in my arms.

We still had no idea what it looked like.

"Juniper, what are we going to do with this puppy?" I asked her again. "How are we going to hide it from Dad?"

Juni knows me. She knew I was desperate. She is not a licker, but she stood on her hind legs and started licking my face. On her hind legs Juniper is almost bigger than me. I am seven years old but short for my age. Juniper knows that when she kisses me she can always make me feel better.

I remember that when I first got Juni I would cry a lot. My Mom and Dad had just gotten divorced, and I was very sad because I missed my Dad when he moved to North Carolina. The tears would start running down my face all the time.

Juniper would come and lick the tears and we would end up laughing and rolling on the floor.

The memory made me smile.

"I love you, Juni." I told her.

It was starting to get light outside. I had to think of something.

It is a good thing that my Dad gets up late, I thought. My Dad is a writer and he writes best late at night so he usually does not get up until around 11AM. That gave me some time to come up with a plan.

First things first, I told myself. We need to get out of the cold. I was barefoot and could hardly feel my toes!

I was trying to think of a solution.

I can't take the puppy inside the house, but we do have a big garage. My Dad hardly ever goes to the garage. I tried to convince myself that everything would be alright.

Just Juniper and I know about the puppy. We will be safe in the garage for now. I told myself.

Chapter 3 – The Note

The puppy was still fast asleep in my arms. I gingerly put him back in the box. I had to go inside the house to open the garage door.

I told Juniper, "Girl, you have to stay outside and watch over the puppy, can you do that?" I could almost hear her say "Yes" as she walked over and stood looking at the box.

I was glad it was almost daylight. People claim to have seen bobcats, coyotes, bears and even a mountain lion roaming around our house!

I am always hoping to see a wild animal, but I have not seen one yet. My Dad saw a mother bear with two cubs last summer. He has been living in the mountains full time for almost two years now, so he has a better chance of seeing wild animals than I do.

I only spend my vacations here with him. The rest of the time I live with my mother in Miami. My mother's family is from Cuba. That's why I have curly black hair and know how to speak Spanish. My Dad is blonde with blue eyes. I really wished my mom was here now. She would know what to do and she would not get mad about the puppy.

I left the puppy with Juniper and went inside the house. I was very quiet, trying to make sure my Dad did not wake up. I looked at the clock as I ran to the garage. It was only 6 AM. It felt like I had been outside for at least three hours! I went into the garage, turned on the lights and looked around trying to figure out the best hiding place.

I opened the garage door and went outside. Juniper had not moved. She looked like a statue guarding the box.

"Good girl!" I said as I hugged her and kissed her. I carefully lifted the box, took it into the garage and placed it in the crawl area under the stairs.

The puppy was still sleeping peacefully.

I saw a paper taped to the side of the box. I had not noticed it before.

I tried to read the note. It was hard for me because it was written in cursive, and very bad cursive at that!

Finally, I was able to decipher it.

Please take care of my puppy. His name is Rocco. I know you will take good care of him. I will be back to get him as soon as I can.

Thanks,

Aiden

I read the note over and over. I could not make out if it said Aiden or Arlen.

"The puppy's name is Rocco, so he is a boy" I told Juniper. I peeked in the box. Rocco was still under the blue flannel shirt, fast asleep. Maybe they will pick him up before Dad wakes up.

I moved my bicycle and Dad's bicycle so they would cover the area where Rocco was sleeping. He was safe for now.

I realized I was starving. "Hungry, girl?" I asked Juniper. She ran to the door and I knew that meant "Yes!"

"Let's go eat" I said, and we tiptoed quietly to the kitchen.

Chapter 4 – The Dilemma

"We must be very quiet Juniper" I told her as I put the food in her dish. She looked at me seriously and I knew she understood.

I gulped down some orange juice and served myself a small bowl of dry cereal.

I wanted to get back to the garage before Rocco woke up.

Juniper must have been thinking the same thing because she finished eating and was standing by the door before I finished drinking my orange juice.

We went inside the garage and sat by the box.

"Juniper, we have a dilemma" I told her petting her. Juni tilted her head to one side and looked at me confused. I could tell she had no idea what I was talking about.

"That's OK, Juni, I know you have never heard that word before," I explained, "a dilemma is when you have to make a very hard decision."

"We have to decide whether to tell Dad about the puppy." I was holding her head and looking into her eyes as I explained to her what the word meant.

Juniper stood up, looked at the box and shook her head from side to side. "No way!" She was telling me.

"Juni, I think you are right. Maybe we should wait until they come and get Rocco." I continued, "we can always tell Dad what happened after he is gone. We can hide him for now."

We were still staring at the blue flannel shirt when Rocco started to wake up. He stretched and the flannel shirt fell off his body. He was so beautiful!

He looked up at us confused, "And who are you?" He seemed to ask.

He started to bark so I picked him up to see if I could keep him quiet. Rocco kept on barking. Juniper started nudging me and trying to get me to go outside. "Woof! Woof!" She barked and ran to the door.

I could tell Juni wanted me to take Rocco outside.

He was wearing a green collar with a metal bone with his name "Rocco" on it. That was good because I could use Juniper's leash to take him out.

"Juni, bring me your leash, please" I asked her. She found her pink leash on the floor and brought it to me. She stood next to me waiting to see what I was going to do.

"Juniper you are right again! I think we have to take Rocco outside to do his business." I explained to her "the last thing we want is for him to make a mess here in the garage and Dad to find it!"

"I know" Juniper seemed to be saying with her eyes, "I remember how mad Dad got when I was a puppy and had an accident inside the house".

Juniper and I took Rocco outside. He was sniffing all around until he found the right spot. Juni was right he had to go!

I figured I should let him run around a little before Dad woke up.

I was really hoping that they would come to pick him up soon. Rocco was beautiful and sweet, but I really needed him to go home before my Dad found out about him. Rocco and Juniper were having fun running around. I was having fun also, but I could tell Juniper was worried. She kept looking at the house. She was worried that my Dad would see Rocco. I was worried also. We played for a while and then we went back to the garage. Rocco went right to sleep on top of the blue flannel shirt. He was exhausted. I remember that Juniper used to sleep a lot when she was a puppy. I looked at the blue flannel shirt. It looked like it belonged to a boy, I thought.

"Juniper, I think the note must say Aiden!" I told her excitedly. "That's a boy's shirt!" I said, proud of my detective work.

"Sophia, Juniper, breakfast is ready!" We heard Dad call from the kitchen. We could smell the bacon cooking.

Juniper looked at Rocco sleeping and then she looked at the door as if asking, "Can we go?"

"Woof! Woof!" She barked. She really loves her bacon.

"Juni, we can go have breakfast but let's eat fast." I told her. "We have to be here when Rocco wakes up to keep him quiet."

Juniper darted into the kitchen. She stood by Dad waiting for her favorite treat.

My Dad makes the best breakfast. I always love to eat breakfast with him because we talk about everything. Today was different. I felt awkward because I knew I was keeping a secret from him.

"Hey, where is my kiss?" He asked me. I always give him a big hug and a kiss. Today I was so preoccupied with Rocco that I just sat down to eat.

"And why are you still wearing your pajamas?" He asked me, "it is 11 o'clock already."

I had not even realized that I was still in my pajamas.

Juniper had gulped down her treat and was standing by the garage door. She was scratching the door and whimpering.

"What is it with her today?" Dad asked looking at Juniper.

"First, she is barking in the middle of the night and now she doesn't want to have breakfast with us. She always begs for more bacon! What is going on?"

"Oh Dad, you know her," I said. "She is just being Juniper!"

Juniper was scratching the door. "I better go with her to the garage to see what she wants" I told Dad.

"That's fine but get dressed so we can go for a hike. It's a beautiful day." Dad said.

I ran into the garage.

"What are we going to do, Juniper?" I asked her. "Dad wants to go on a hike!"

I heard the cellphone ringing inside the house. I knew by the ring that it was Mom. "Sophie, your phone is ringing!" Dad called from the kitchen.

"Juni, watch Rocco! I have to run and get the phone before Dad brings it in here" I said as I ran in the house. I was back in a flash with my cell phone in my hand.

"Hi Mom" I answered the phone.

When I heard my Mom's voice I wanted to tell her all about Rocco and the note. She must have heard the worry in my voice because she asked me right away, "Sophia, what is the matter? What's wrong? You sound worried," she kept insisting.

I blurted everything out. "Mom, they left a puppy in a box outside the house! We are hiding it! We haven't even told Dad"

"What?" My mom asked.

"Yes, and they left a note and his name is Rocco and he is a Golden just like Juniper. Mom, what do I do?" I asked her, "I wish you were here!"

"I wish I was there too," my Mom said. "Sophia, you must tell your Dad. You have not done anything wrong. He may even know who this boy Aiden is and where he lives."

She convinced me. I had not thought of the possibility that my Dad might know who Rocco belonged to.

"Mom, I will tell him, but I am worried. Remember how he would say that Juniper would be nothing but trouble!" I told her.

I was still scared of Dad seeing Rocco, but I knew I had to tell him.

Chapter 5 – Telling Dad

"Sophie, Juniper!" Let's go on that hike!" called Dad.

I took a deep breath and walked out of the garage. Dad was standing outside ready to go. I walked up to him.

"Dad, we have a problem" I told him seriously. He looked at me with a worried look on his face.

"What is it Sophie? What's the matter?" He asked.

I took Dad by the hand and went into the garage. Juniper looked at me as if I was crazy. "What are you doing?!" She seemed to be asking.

Rocco was up. He was playing with Juniper's favorite toy, the red monkey. He ran to my Dad!

"Oh no!" I thought.

My dad looked at me, then he looked at Juniper and then he looked at Rocco. He was speechless.

"This is Rocco" I said as I handed him the note that was on the box.

He looked at me sternly, "When did this happen?" He asked.

"We found him under the rose bushes this morning" I told him. "He was in that box" I said pointing to the cardboard box.

"That's why Juni was barking today." I explained, "she led me to the box and the puppy".

"You went out by yourself in the middle of the night?" He was mad now. "I have told you never to do that!" "Just last week Bob claims he saw a mountain lion roaming around".

"I'm sorry Dad, we will not do it again, I promise." I replied.

Juniper came and stood by my side, giving me moral support.

Dad read the note again. "Sophia, who is this Aiden? He asked. "When is he coming to pick up this dog?"

My Dad hardly ever calls me Sophia. He always calls me Sophie. I knew he was upset.

"Dad, I don't know who he is." I said almost crying. "That is why I told you we had a problem!"

"What do you mean you don't know who he is?!" He was exasperated now.

"Dad, they probably had an emergency and they did not want to leave the puppy home alone." I tried to sound convincing. "I am sure they will pick him up in a little while".

"Let's hope so!" He said, "because this dog is not staying here!"

Rocco was running around the garage, oblivious to the conversation.

He was jumping on Juniper, trying to get her to play with him but she was ignoring him. Juniper's gaze was fixed on my Dad, intent on understanding what was going to happen with Rocco.

"Daddy, we can't go on a hike now, we need to be here when they pick the puppy up," I said. "Maybe we can go hiking this afternoon after he is gone? Is that OK?"

"We'll see" He said. He was very serious. I could tell he was upset but he wasn't yelling.

My Dad never yells. The only time I have heard him yell was when he was really mad at my Mom because she wanted a divorce. He was very mad and very sad then. I was also very, very sad.

I was so sad that I think that is why my Mom got me Juniper. I guess sometimes good things can come from bad things.

"Sophia, I am going to my study to try to get some work done," Dad told me, "If they come to pick up that dog you need to get me. I want to speak to that boy and his family."

"Sure, Dad," I replied.

I decided I might as well play with the puppy while he was here.

"Juni, let's go out to play" Juniper ran out the door. Rocco ran after her.

They were both so beautiful!

Rocco was chasing Juniper and biting her. Juniper was loving it.

"Here Rocco!" I called him. He came right over. "Smart puppy!" I said as I petted him.

Soon the three of us were on the grass rolling around. Juniper licking my face. Rocco trying to bite me. He was playing, of course. I was on the floor laughing.

The afternoon went by too fast. I guess it's true that time flies when you are having fun!

I went to the kitchen to grab an apple. I looked at the time. It was already 4 o'clock. I went back outside. Juniper and Rocco both ran up to me. I started running so they would chase me.

My father came outside. "Sophie" he said, "We need to talk."

"Ok" I said, worried.

"Take the puppy and Juniper to the garage and give them some water first. They must be thirsty." He said.

"Come here girl!" I called. Juniper ran to me with Rocco at her heels. "Let's have some water."

Dad was right. They were both thirsty and exhausted from so much running and playing.

They laid down and went to sleep. I closed the garage door and went to talk to my father.

Chapter 6 – The Plan

"Sophie, come sit next to me." Dad was sitting on the sofa waiting for me.

At least he is calling me "Sophie" I thought.

I sat next to him. "Sophie, you know we cannot keep Rocco."

"I know Dad, I don't want to keep Rocco. I am happy with just Juniper. The note said that they are going to come pick him up soon."

"Sophie, the note said, "as soon as I can", what does that even mean?" Dad asked.

Dad was holding me close as he spoke. "We will keep Rocco overnight but if they have not picked him up by 3PM tomorrow we are going to take him to "Admirals Pet Adoption Center." I already spoke to Liz and Viv about the puppy," Dad continued.

Liz and Viv are good friends of Dad. They do volunteer work at Admirals, and they have two Goldens who are Juniper's friends.

"You know Liz and Viv will find the best home for him." He reassured me.

"But Dad he has an owner! You read the note! Aiden says he will pick him up as soon as he can!" I begged "We can keep him a few more days to see if he comes to get him."

"Sophie, the puppy may have a chip that tells us who the owners are and where they live. The vet at Admirals will try to locate them."

Dad was right about that. Juniper has a chip in case she ever gets lost.

"Sophie, tonight you may even bring Rocco inside and he can sleep with you and Juniper. Tomorrow, we have to try to find his owners."

"Is that a deal?" He asked me.

"Alright Dad" I said, still not happy about taking Rocco to Admirals Pet Adoption Center.

He hugged me and told me, "Now go to the garage and bring Juniper and the puppy inside so they can have something to eat. I will start making dinner for us. How about some Mac and Cheese?" Dad knew it was my favorite.

After we had dinner, my Dad watched the News on TV. I sat on the floor brushing Juniper with Rocco snuggling next to me. I kept hoping that Aiden would show up at the door.

They had entrusted this puppy to me, and it was just wrong to take it to Admirals Pet Adoption Center tomorrow!

I had to find a solution!

Dad interrupted my thoughts, "Let's take Juniper and Rocco out one last time before bedtime. Make sure you put the puppy on a leash. You don't want him getting far from us."

When we came back from the short walk Juniper and Rocco were both tired. The three of us climbed into bed. I was asleep before my head hit the pillow.

The sun woke me up.

I looked at the time on my phone. It was only 7AM.

I was still very upset about taking Rocco to the pet adoption center today.

I had to think of a way to keep him safe until someone came to pick him up.

Juniper and Rocco were both sleeping soundly next to me.

Finally, I thought of something!

I don't like to lie to my Dad... but my idea could work, I told myself. I can hide Rocco in our favorite secret place!... in the cave!

Chapter 7 – The Cave

I was still in bed trying to figure out what to do. Could we really hide Rocco in the cave? How about at night?!!!

I can't leave him in the cave alone at night. I worried.

"Maybe Gaby can help me figure out what to do?" I was talking to myself. I talk to myself when I am confused or worried.

The cave is down the hill from our house. It is off the road and not visible at all. It is a small cave where Juniper and I go to play all the time.

We live on Deer Trail Road. There are only five houses on Deer Trail Road and our house is the highest one on the mountain. There are no houses beyond ours.

When Aiden comes to pick up Rocco he will have to walk near the cave before he gets to the house. Gaby and I will be able to see him from the cave.

My brain was going non-stop planning everything we had to do.

"Juniper! Juniper! Wake up! I have a plan!" she looked at me and tried to go back to sleep, "Juni, you have to get up! This is serious!"

Juniper sat up on the bed and looked at Rocco asleep next to her, "Why can he sleep?" She was asking.

I put on my jeans and my favorite red T-shirt. I looked for my hiking boots in the closet. Juniper was looking at me and looking at the boots.

"Hiking so early?" She seemed to be asking. She started wagging her tail and getting excited. She loves to go hiking! "Woof! Woof!" Juni was ready to go.

"Not yet girl" I told her. "Soon, but we have a lot to do first".

Rocco woke up and started barking "I gotta go!" He was trying to say. He was running to the door.

"Juni, let's take Rocco out fast!" I said as I ran down the stairs. Rocco almost tripped me. He was going so fast I was afraid he was going to roll down the stairs.

We went out the front door. Rocco was right. He had to go!

Juniper started running up and down the hill. She wanted me to chase her.

We do this every morning, just for fun.

After a while I was winded and sat on one of the rocking chairs on the front porch while Juniper and Rocco played.

I felt bad about lying to Dad, but I saw no
other way!

It was chilly outside. It was already the
second week of June but in the
mountains it got cold early in the
morning and late at night.
My Dad said he didn't think it was cold at
all, but it felt cold to me.
"That's because you are a Miami girl!" He
would tell me lovingly every time I
complained about the cold.
"Breakfast is ready!" Dad was calling us.
 It seemed early for Dad to be up. He was
probably worried about Rocco also.
We sat down for breakfast. Juniper got a
piece of bacon.

Rocco got a piece of bacon also. He loved it!

I took a deep breath and said, "Dad, I have a plan."
"A plan?" He asked.

(Of course, I was not going to tell him about the cave!)

Juniper looking at me, she was trying to figure out what I was going to say. I was petting her as I talked. Petting her always calmed me. I needed to be calm now.

"Dad, we really have not tried to find Rocco's owner. Maybe someone who lives on the mountain knows him. I think we should ask around today before we take him to Admirals."

"OK, that makes sense." He replied.

"Dad, I can stay here with Juniper in case someone shows up to pick Rocco up. You can go in the truck and ask around. Maybe you can even go to the the grocery store and see if someone knows Rocco. Take a picture of him with your phone and show his picture to everyone."

"Sophie, that actually sounds like a good idea." He said, "the only part I don't like is you staying by yourself here all that time."

I knew he was going to say that. I had a solution.

"I can call Gaby. She can come over and stay with me. Gaby has not even met Rocco yet. You know how much she loves Goldens!"

Gaby was my very best friend. She lives in Miami, like me. Her mother and my mom teach in the same school. Gaby and I have been in the same class since kindergarten. It was because of her family that my parents bought the house in North Carolina. Gaby's Mom and Dad bought their house first. One summer they invited us to stay with them for a week. My Mom fell in love with North Carolina and six months later my Mom and Dad bought our house.

Now it is my Dad's house but at the beginning it was our house. We came in the summer, at Christmas and for Spring Break. When they got divorced my Dad moved here full time.

I am very lucky because I get to spend lots of time with my best friend Gaby, both in Miami and in North Carolina.

I knew Gaby would help me.

"OK," he said, "call Gabriela. The two of you can take Rocco around some of the nearby houses to see if anyone knows him."

I took my cellphone out of my back pocket and texted Gaby. "Can u come over fast? I need your help! Wear your hiking boots."

"What's wrong? I will be there in a minute. Let me tell Mom." she texted me back right away.

Gaby lives three houses down, just a short way down the hill.

"Gaby is coming right over," I told my father.

I felt guilty because he believed everything, I had told him. He did not know the other part to my plan.

I was going to hide Rocco in the cave!

"OK then I will go in the truck and canvass the neighboring areas just in case someone knows Rocco or that boy, Aiden," he said.

"Rocco! Come over for a picture!" he called. Rocco ran over to my Dad. He was one smart puppy. Juniper ran to my Dad also. She loves pictures and poses for the camera.

"OK Girl! I'll take a picture of you too!" Dad laughed as he took pictures of Rocco and a picture of Juniper.

"Dad, we should leave a note on the door in case someone comes to pick up Rocco

while we are out searching for his owners"
I said.

"Yes, Sophie, you are right. Go write the note and I'll tape it to the door"
I ran to the kitchen and wrote the note:

We are out searching for Rocco's owner. If you are his owner and came to pick him up please call us immediately.
Please call Frank at 305-551-0431 or Sophie at 305-714-1111
Thanks,
Sophia

"Sophie, I'm not sure I want your number there" he said when he read it. "I don't want you dealing with strangers".
"But Dad, what if they call and you don't hear the phone?" I pleaded.
I needed my number on the note because we were not going to be home.
We were going to be in the cave hiding Rocco!
"Fine but promise to call me right away if anyone calls you. And promise you will be with Gabriela and Juniper the entire

time." Dad said as he took the note and taped it to the front door.

I saw Gaby running up the hill.

"Oh no! What a beautiful puppy!" I heard Gaby screaming when she saw Rocco.

"Juniper, who is your new friend?! Where did you get him?! When did you get him?!" she screamed as she petted Juniper and Rocco.

Gaby was so excited, "Sophia, you are sooooo lucky! Two Goldens!"

Gaby ran up to me and hugged me and was jumping up at down.

"Why didn't you tell me?!" She exclaimed.

"Gaby, he is not mine. I can't keep him. I will explain everything in a sec," I told her.

"Sophie, I will drive around and try to find Rocco's owners first but remember that we have an appointment at Admirals at 4PM today." Dad reminded me. "Liz will be there to do all the paperwork. She will try to find his owners or find him a good home."

Dad got in his truck, "See you later sweetheart! Let's hope I get some information about Rocco." He said as he drove away.

"Bye Dad!" I waived to him.
Juniper stood next to me. She seemed as nervous as I was.

Chapter 8 – Hiding Rocco

"Gaby, we have to hide Rocco in the cave!"
I told her excitedly.
"What?!" Gaby's eyes opened wide.
Juniper kept staring at me and barking in
agreement, but you could tell she was
scared.
"Everything will be fine Juniper! You'll
see," I told her and kissed her.
"What do you mean we have to hide him
in the cave?! Why?!" Gaby kept asking.
"My Dad is going to take him to the
Adoption Center today!" I was almost
crying as I told her about the note and how
I had found Rocco in the box.
"Oh no!" Gaby agreed. "Sophie, of course
you have to hide him. You can't take him
to Admirals. They trusted you to take care
of him!"
"OK then, we have to get to work," I said
"Juni, Gaby, we have to move fast!"
"We have to make sure that we take
everything Rocco will need to the cave."
"We have to take his food, lots of water, his
cardboard box, the blue flannel shirt. Let's
go!" I was nervous but excited.
We ran to the garage.

"Juni, can you take a toy for Rocco?" I
asked her.
Juniper picked up her favorite toy, the red
monkey.

"I'll take the water and the food," Gaby said as she picked up a gallon of water.

"Gaby, give me the food. I can put it inside the cardboard box with the flannel shirt and a tennis ball," I could see that the gallon of water was very heavy, "just take the water." I told her as I put the food in the box.

We ran down the street until we got to a big maple tree. Juniper knew exactly where we were going. She was leading the way. Rocco was barking and trying hard to keep up with her.

When she got to the cave she stopped. "Woof! Woof! We are here!"

We went inside the cave. It was a small cave but perfect for us.

We put everything down. Juniper and Rocco were playing and barking. They just loved the cave.

I was worried about the noise. "I am going to run to the road to see if I can see or hear anything from there," I told Gaby.

When I got to the road the only thing I could see were the outcrop of rocks above the cave. Nothing else.

I listened carefully. I could not hear the dogs. I called Gaby on the phone. I did not even hear the phone ringing.

"Gaby, have Juniper and Rocco barked at all?" I asked her when she answered.

"Yes, they are playing and barking in the area right below the cave," she said.

"Good! I can't hear or see anything!" I told her and ran back to the cave.

This may work. I told myself. The hardest part is going to be lying to my Dad!

When I got back to the cave the phone rang. "Oh no, it's Mom" I said.

"You can't answer!" Gaby screamed. "She'll know! Moms know everything! You better just text her."

I decided Gaby was right. Mom would figure out that something strange was going on if I spoke to her.

"Mom, I can't talk now. I will call u later" I texted her.

"OK" she replied, "don't forget to call me."

That was easy, I thought.

Maybe I can text Dad instead of telling him. It will be easier to lie to him about Rocco getting picked up if I don't have to talk to him.

"Gaby, I hope they pick Rocco up this weekend, either today or tomorrow. They can't just leave him here forever!" I was frantic.

"I'm sure they will pick him up soon," Gaby said trying to calm me.

"Very soon I am going to have to text Dad and lie to him and tell him that they just picked up Rocco," I told Gaby nervously. I was scared.

"Gaby, how are we going to do this? We can't leave Rocco in the cave by himself at night! He is just a puppy!" I said almost crying.

"Sophie, I have an idea!" Gaby screamed. "We can all sleep in the cave together!"

"How are we going to do that?!" I asked.

"My Dad will miss me and Juniper and your Mom and Dad will miss you."

"I have it all figured out. I will tell my Mom that I am going to sleep over at your house!" Gaby said excitedly. "You tell your Dad that you are going to sleep over at my house. That way they will not miss either one of us!"

"Gaby, that's brilliant!" You are right! Our parents won't miss us at all!"

Sleeping in the cave would be scary but we had to do it.

"We are going to have to find a way to cover the opening of the cave. It is dangerous at night." I said.

Gaby was scared also. I could tell by the look on her face.

"How can we cover the opening of the cave?" I asked out loud.

"Woof! Woof!" Juniper started barking. She ran up the hill to the house.

I knew she wanted me to follow her.

"Gaby stay here with Rocco. Juniper has an idea!" I ran up the hill with Juniper.

She stopped by the side of the house. I could not believe my eyes!

"Juni! I love you! You are so smart!" I hugged her and kissed her.

Juniper stood by a huge piece of cardboard. Just two days ago they had delivered a brand new two door refrigerator. Juniper had found the perfect door for our cave!!!

"Juni, can you help me take it to the cave?" I asked her.

Carefully we dragged the huge box down the hill and to the cave.

"That's perfect!" Gaby screamed when she saw the big piece of cardboard. "We will be safe now!"

"Text your Dad now and tell him they picked up Rocco." Gaby told me, "Just do it."

"OK, here goes" I said as I started texting. *"Daddy, I have great news. They just picked up the puppy."* I was breathless, waiting for his reply.

"Great" He texted back *"what's the story?"* He asked.

"It's a long story," I replied. *"I will tell you when I see you. Can Juniper and I sleep over at Gaby's tonight?"* I texted him.

"Sure, at what time do I pick you up tomorrow?" He asked me.

"After lunch, around 3:30. Is that OK? "I replied.

"That's fine. I will pick you up at Gabriela's at 3:30 tomorrow," he texted me. *"I am so glad everything turned out well with the puppy. Be good* at Gabriela's and have fun!"

I felt horrible lying to my Dad.

"Gaby, what a mess!" I was crying now, "we really need Aiden to show up right now!"

"Sophie don't worry. We will figure something out." Gaby hugged me. "We always do!"

Chapter 9 – DANGER!!!

"Dad's calling!" I panicked when I heard his ring again, "what do I do?" I asked Gaby.

"You have to answer the phone," Gaby said seriously, "we don't want him getting suspicious."

"Hi Daddy" I answered.

"Sophie, I just wanted to remind you to call your mother," he said, "she called me earlier and I forgot to tell you."

I breathed a sigh of relief!

"What's all that barking?" he asked. "Just Juniper?"

"Yes, it's just Juniper." I said.

"Don't forget to call your mother" He reminded me again, "see you tomorrow and tell Juniper to stop barking!"

I saw Rocco and Juniper playing and barking by the cave. They were having such fun. No wonder Dad could hear them!

"Gaby, I have to run to the house before Dad gets back. I am going to bring his big sleeping bag, a flashlight, bread, and peanut butter and jelly." I told her as I ran up the hill. "Can you think of anything else we need?"

"Maybe some chips and some rope." Gaby said "We need to secure the cardboard to the opening of the cave somehow. We need to be safe at night."

"Yes, it's too scary," I agreed.

"Juni, come with me!" I called her. "I need your help bringing stuff down to the cave." Juniper looked at me and ran ahead. She was always anxious to help.

We went straight to the kitchen. I got the food and some treats for Juni and Rocco. I put the food and the flashlight in my book bag. Then I got the sleeping bag and the rope.

"Juni, come help!" she came right over and I put the rope around her neck. "Juniper hold this part in your mouth so you don't get tangled" I told her.

"Good girl!" I said as she opened her mouth to hold the rope.

"Juni, let's go! We have to get out of here before Dad gets back home!"

She ran down the hill so fast she was a blur of gold.

"Did you get everything we need?" Gaby asked when we got back to the cave.

"Yes, I think so" I answered

We were excited but also nervous. Juniper
was scared too. Rocco was just having fun.

"Sophie, come help me move those two big
rocks," Gaby pointed, "we can use them to
hold the bottom of the cardboard in place.
The opening of the cave has to be
completely covered for us to be safe at
night."
"Yes, you are right." I told her as we
moved the rocks. I was terrified of
sleeping in the cave. "We have to make
sure the cave is safe."
We covered the opening of the cave with
the big cardboard. We were both standing
outside the cave. I held the cardboard in
place. Gaby secured it with the big rocks
on the bottom. It was secure on the
bottom, but it kept flipping over from the
top.
"Gaby, go around to the other side of the
cave." I said excitedly, "I will throw the
rope over the rocks. I think we can use the
rope to tie down the top of the cardboard."

We finally managed to tie the rope around the outcrop of rocks.
It worked! The cave opening was completely closed!
It looked very secure.
"I think it will be safe to sleep inside the cave now." I said satisfied.
Immediately I realized that we had a big problem.
We were standing outside of the cave!

"Oh no! We can't get inside!" I said.
Juniper came over and looked at us and looked at the cave. She looked very perplexed.
Gaby and I could not help but laugh.

"'Yes girl," I said laughing "The cave is safe and perfectly shut but we can't get inside!"
Juni went over to the cave, "Woof! Woof!"

"Yes, we can!" She seemed to say.
She started to show us how! She was digging a tunnel under the cardboard.
Dirt was flying all over. Juniper was digging fast. She was full of dirt. We had dirt all over us also.

"Juniper, slow down!" I said brushing the dirt away from my face. "We are going to get dirt in our eyes!"

Juni was determined.

In no time at all she had dug the perfect tunnel under the cardboard.

Gaby said "Leave it to Juniper! She can always figure out what to do!"

"Juni, come here!" I hugged her. "You are the smartest, sweetest, best dog in the world!"

I kept kissing her, "Juniper you are just perfect!"

She looked at me very seriously, "I'm Just Juniper," she seemed to say.

We stayed outside the cave until it began to get dark.

"I think we should go inside now. I will go in first so I can call Rocco." I crawled in through the tunnel Juniper had dug.

"Rocco, come in boy! Come in the cave!" I put a treat in my hand and put my hand through the tunnel. Rocco came right in. "Good boy! Here is your treat."

"Juni, come here girl!" I hardly had to call her. She knew exactly what to do.

Gaby crawled in last.

"Juniper, you can fill the hole back in now." Juniper filled in the tunnel really fast.

I think she wanted to make sure we were safe inside the cave.

"It is dark in here now!" Gaby said, "Where is the flashlight?"

"Here Gaby, you keep the flashlight." I told her.

It was getting cold so we climbed into the sleeping bag. Juniper and Rocco snuggled next to us.

"This is scary but it is also very, very exciting!" I told Gaby.

She agreed. We started to giggle.

It was a nervous giggle. It was contagious. The more I giggled the more Gaby giggled. Suddenly we heard a noise outside!

"Grrrr! Grrrr!"

We froze and stopped giggling. Juniper got closer to me.

Rocco started to bark.

"Quiet boy," I whispered as I pulled him into the sleeping bag.

"Go to sleep Rocco." I told him.

I could feel Gaby trembling next to me.

We heard the noise again!

"Grrrr! Grrrr!"

It sounded like something was scratching the cardboard outside.

Juniper got up. She was looking towards the opening.

"It is trying to come inside the cave!" I whispered to Gaby.

"Grrrr! Grrrrr!"

It sounded mad! Whatever it was, it was pounding and scratching the cardboard!

"It wants to come inside." Gaby was crying now.

Juniper started walking toward the opening of the cave.

"No girl, stay here!" I whispered, "Juni, it's OK, we just have to be quiet," I explained as I petted her.

"Come in here," I said as I made room for her in the sleeping bag.

She licked my face but would not come into the sleeping bag. She laid down on the floor next to the sleeping bag. Her stare frozen on the cardboard door.

The sound continued. "Grrrr! Grrrr!"

"Turn off the flashlight" I whispered to Gaby.

She looked at me terrified. Gaby was afraid of the dark.

It was pitch black in the cave now.

I held Gaby close. I was very afraid, but I had to be brave for Gaby.

After all, this was all my doing.

I was the one who got us into this mess!

"Juni, come here" I whispered. Petting Juniper always made me feel better. I could not see her in the dark but I could feel her warmth. I needed her to make me feel better now.

"Grrrr!" We heard more growling

"GRRRR! GRRRR!" The growling was getting louder and louder.

"GRRRR! GRRRR!"

Whatever it was really wanted to come inside!
What if the cave was their home?

I was worried.

"GRRRR! GRRRR!"

We held our breath. We did not want to make a sound. After a long while it got quiet.
"That was too scary!" I whispered to Gaby "Let's try to get some sleep now"
"Can I at least keep the flashlight on?" Gaby asked me.
"OK" I whispered, "but keep it inside the sleeping bag and don't wake up Rocco!"
The wind started howling outside. It felt like the cardboard box was going to fly away!
"Haooooo!"   "Haoooooo!"

Oh no! What now? I wondered.
"What is that?!!!" Gaby asked me.
"I don't know Gaby, it sounds like a coyote or maybe a wolf?" I told her as I held her close.
 "It sounds like it is far away" I reassured her.
"Haoooooo! Haooooooo!

We heard the sound again.

"Maybe it is just the wind!" I said hopefully. "Or maybe it's an owl!"
"Haoooooo! Haoooooo! Haooooo!!"
The sound was louder now!
"Haoooooo! Haoooooo!"

"I think it may just be the wind." I tried to reassure Gaby.
"It feels like the wind is going to lift the cardboard right off!" Gaby was crying now.
What if the cardboard was blown away?!
The thought terrified me.
Any wild animal could come in the cave and attack us.

Juniper was scared too! She finally climbed into the sleeping bag next to me.

"It's OK girl" I whispered in her ear as I hugged her, "it's just the wind."

The sound continued for a very long time.
Finally, it got very quiet.

We were exhausted from fear!
Eventually we fell asleep.

The next thing I remember is hearing a loud sound!

Boom!

It sounded like an explosion!

It was Juniper bursting out of the cardboard door!

She jumped right through the cardboard box, ripping it apart and running outside!

Rocco was running after her!

Bright sunlight came into the cave. It was already morning.

"Juniper! What are you doing?!" I called her. "Juniper, Stop!"

She was running down the hill like a maniac.

Rocco was running after her!

Chapter 10– Juniper Saves the Day!

"Juniper, Stop! I yelled as I ran up the hill after her, "STOP!"

I saw a red car parked in our driveway.

A white-haired lady was getting out of the driver's seat.

Two boys were sitting in the back seat of the car.

Juniper was running so fast that I could not catch up to her. She ran past the red car. Rocco stopped running when he got to the red car. The two boys started calling him, "Come here Rocco!"

"Come here boy!" the boys opened the car door and Rocco jumped right in. He started licking the boys.

I was running up the hill when I saw Rocco get into the car with the two boys. That must be Aiden. He is coming to pick up Rocco. I breathed a sigh of relief.

"Oh no!" I screamed as I continued running. If the lady talks to Dad he would know I lied to him! He can't find out we slept in the cave!

Juniper got to the front door of our house just as the white-haired lady was knocking on the door.

740

She almost knocked the lady down!

I realized what Juniper was trying to do. Juni was trying to distract Dad to save me!

She was not going to let the lady talk to Dad.
She knew I would be dead meat if my Dad found out I had lied to him.
She knew I would be grounded for the rest of my life if he found out that we slept in the cave!
Dad opened the front door. "May I help you...?" He could not finish the sentence. Juniper jumped on him and started licking him.

"Juniper, stop! What are you doing here?" He asked her, "where is Sophia?"

"Excuse me ma'am" He was speaking to the white-haired lady now "I don't know what's come over her. She never acts this way! She is usually very well behaved."
"JUNIPER STOP!" He was mad now. Juniper would not stop. She kept jumping and licking his face.

"She is just showing you how much she loves you," The lady said.

Juniper calmed down. She looked at the lady and then looked at Dad.

"I just wanted to come by to thank you for taking care of Rocco. My name is Anna" she continued. "I am Tom Hewey's sister. I am staying at his house for a couple of weeks. Those are my two grandsons in the car, Aiden and Ben in the car."

Dad looked towards the red car. Rocco was in the back seat playing with the two boys. I had stopped running and was standing by the car talking to them.

"Glad we could help" he said to the white-haired lady. "That's what neighbors are for."
"Maybe your daughter and Juniper can come over to play with the boys later?" asked Anna
Juniper looked at Anna and wagged her tail.
"That'll be fine, but Juniper better behave!" Dad said looking sternly at Juniper.
"I'm sure she will" Anna said as she petted Juniper.
"See you later then. Thanks again for taking care of Rocco," she said as she walked towards her car.
Juniper was standing by my Dad with a satisfied look on her face.

She had accomplished her goal!

Dad still believed Aiden had picked up Rocco yesterday!

When Dad saw Rocco he was already inside the car playing with the two boys.

Of course, Dad would think that Rocco came in the car with them. He thought they had picked him up the day before.

It made perfect sense that Anna, Aiden's grandmother would come over to meet him and thank him personally.

Juniper was a genius! I thought proudly.

"Sophia!" Dad called me, "You better talk to your dog! I don't know what is going on with her. She almost knocked down that lady.
Juniper has never acted like this. She has never jumped up on me before!"
"Oh Dad, don't be mean. She just got excited to see you." I told him petting Juniper.
"And just look at her!" He said sternly.
"Why is she so dirty?" He looked at Juniper and then looked at me.

"You are a mess also!"

"How come you are back so early?" he continued, "we agreed that I was going to go get you after lunch. Where is Gabriela?"

I had forgotten all about Gaby!
She must still be sleeping in the cave!!!

"Gaby is coming right over" I said looking at Juniper, "Aiden texted me that they were coming over with Rocco" I was lying to my Dad again! "I wanted to be here when they got here."

I wanted to make sure he believed that Rocco had been picked up yesterday. My Dad could not find out we slept in the cave.

"The first thing you are doing is getting Juniper ready for a bath. She is not allowed in the house until she is clean." Dad told me.

Juniper heard him and started wagging her tail. Juniper loves water!

I guess she takes after me. My favorite thing in the world is the ocean. We go swimming all the time when we are in Miami.

Juni loves the ocean, but I think she loves the hose just as much!

"Have you had breakfast yet?" My Dad asked, "I can make pancakes for you and Gaby, but first you and Juniper have to take a bath."

I saw Gaby running up the hill. She must have just woken up, I thought.

Gaby was screaming, "What happened?! Where did everyone go?! Where is Rocco?! Why did you leave me alone in the cave?!!!!!"

I ran down the hill to meet her. I ran as fast as I could. Juniper came running after me.

"Gaby wait there!" I told her. I could not let her get near the house and keep asking questions in front of Dad.

Gaby was more of a mess than I was. Her hair was tangled and full of dirt. Her jeans and frilly pink shirt full of stains.

I could not let my Dad see Gaby like that.

He would know for sure that something weird was going on.

Gaby was never messy. She was a very girly girl. Always very neat and color coordinated.
I grabbed Gaby by the shoulders and whispered to her, "You have to calm down and listen carefully," I explained to her exactly what had happened.

"Huh?!" "What?!" "Rocco is gone?!" "I can't believe I slept through the whole thing!" She screamed.

"Shhhh," I warned her. "Dad can't find out. He can never find out we slept in the cave!"
Dad was by the garage getting everything ready for Juniper's bath.
"Gaby go ask your Mom if you can have breakfast with us." I said loudly so Dad would hear me. "Dad is going to make pancakes for us."
"Huh?" She whispered. "Huh? Sophie, don't you remember my parents think I

slept over at your house?! I can't just show up at my house now." She reminded me.

"Gaby, you are right," I whispered. "I forgot. But you are going to have to sneak into your house somehow without your parents seeing you. You must change your clothes."

Gaby looked at herself, "I am a mess! Don't worry I'll find a way to sneak into my house. I will be back in no time" she said as she ran home.

Juniper was standing next to us, listening intently. "Girl, you saved my life today!" I whispered as I hugged her.

"You are a genius." I told her proudly.

She stood on her hind legs and started licking me.

Then she stopped and got that serious look on her face "A genius?" She was asking with her eyes.

She barked, "No, I'm Just Juniper!" I knew she was telling me.

"OK, OK" I told her, "You are Just Juniper!"

"But you are incredible and fantastic, and I love you!" I hugged her again and again.

Chapter 11 – New Friends

"Juniper! Sophie! Come get cleaned up."

Dad called us from the side of the house. Juniper saw the hose in his hand.

She was up the hill and in the water in two seconds flat.

"Slow down girl. Let me soap you" my father was trying to get Juniper to stop playing in the water. "You are really dirty. How did you get so dirty?" he asked her.

Juniper looked at me, "If you only knew!!!" She seemed to say.
I looked away. I had to laugh at the expression on her face.

 "Sophie, go take a bath yourself. I will bathe Juniper" my Dad said. "You are as dirty as she is."
When I came down the stairs my Dad said, "Now, that's much better." He handed me the blow dryer and told me "You blow dry and brush Juniper. I am going to make breakfast."

Soon we could hear the bacon sizzling. The smell of bacon made me realize I was starving. We had been so terrified last night that we forgot to eat.

"I'm here!" Gaby said knocking at the door.
"Come in Gabriela. The door is open" my Dad said
I was still brushing Juniper when Gaby walked in.
Gaby was back to her own self. Her beautiful hair was up in a ponytail. It was tied with a pink bow matching her pink t-shirt and her pink tennis shoes.
"It smells yummy!" She told my Dad. "Thank you for inviting me over for breakfast."
Gaby was always very polite.
"I know how much you love pancakes, Gaby," he said "You know we love to have you here."
The pancakes were delicious. My Dad loves to cook. He is a much better cook than my Mom.
Gaby ate a huge stack of pancakes. Gaby is tiny, but she eats like a horse.

We were still having breakfast when I heard my Dad's phone ringing. I heard Dad talking to Mom.

"Ellie, don't be mad at me. Talk to your daughter!" I heard him say, "I told her to call you."

I knew she was complaining because I did not call her last night. With all the excitement I completely forgot.

"Sophia! Your mother wants to speak to you," Dad gave me his cellphone.

"Mommy, I'm so sorry I forgot to call you last night." I did not give her chance to speak. I knew that my Mom would forgive me if I apologized and called her Mommy. "Please forgive me. I will never forget to call you again. I promise!"

"Sophia, stop with the drama!" Mom told me, "I was just worried because you were so distraught about the puppy" she continued, "Did the boy finally pick him up?"

"Yes everything is fine Mom. Everything worked out."

"Good. Call me tonight. Don't forget. I love you." She said.

"I love you too Mom." I said as I hung up, "Dad, can we go over to see Rocco and the boys now?" I asked.

I wanted to find out why Aiden had left Rocco in a box at our house in the middle of the night. I needed to know everything before my Dad asked me questions.

Sooner or later Dad was going to ask, and I better have some answers.

"Sure, but make sure that Juniper behaves," He replied. "She acted crazy this morning!"

Tom Hewey's cabin is close to Gaby's house. We had to walk down the hill past the cave.

"That was so scary last night!" We exclaimed as we left the cave behind.

Juniper barked in agreement.

Rocco saw us first. He was barking and running towards us. Ben and Aiden saw us and waived.

"Hi Aiden! Hi Ben!" I said. "This is Gaby, my best friend."

"Hi!" They all said at the same time.

"Aiden, we need to talk." I said seriously.

"OK?" He replied.

"We have a problem" I continued, "My Dad was very upset about Rocco. He was going to take him to the pet adoption center yesterday."

Gaby interrupted, "We had to hide him and sleep in the cave!"

"What cave?!" Ben asked excitedly. "You slept in a cave?!"

"Gaby, let me explain everything to Aiden first" I said patiently.

Aiden was listening quietly. "What happened?" He asked.

I explained everything.

"You really slept in a cave?!" Aiden exclaimed in disbelief.

His eyes got wider and wider as I told him about the animal trying to get inside the cave.

His jaw dropped as he listened to what a close call we had last night.

"Aiden, my father can't know any of this!" I begged. "Maybe I will tell him in a few years when I am older."

It was hard thinking I would never tell my Dad the truth.

"I can't tell him right now." I said.

"OK, I understand," he said seriously.

I looked down. I was ashamed of myself. I hated lying to my Dad and my Mom. I wished I could tell them the truth.

"Aiden, I need you to tell me why you left Rocco outside my house that night?" I asked "My father is going to want to know."

"Sophie, this is what happened. We had just gotten to the mountains three days before. We are city boys, we live in New York City, so we are not the best mountain climbers," Aiden explained. "I'm pretty athletic but my brother Ben is sort of clumsy."

"What?" complained Ben, "I am not clumsy! The rocks were slippery!"

"It was late in the afternoon, and we were climbing on the rocks behind the house and Ben fell down." Aiden continued.

"My grandmother had to rush him to the hospital. She let me stay home with Rocco only because she thought they would be coming right back."

"I broke my arm!" Ben interrupted pointing to the cast on his arm.

"Yes, I figured it had something to do with Ben's broken arm when I saw the cast," I said.

"Yes," explained Aiden. "When they got to the hospital, they told Ben he had to stay overnight. He had a compound fracture and needed surgery. Ben has a heart condition and doctors are very careful when treating him."

"My grandmother was frantic," continued Aiden, "I told her not to worry and stay in the hospital with Ben, that I was fine at home with Rocco."

"Grandma would not allow it. She told me she would come pick me up as soon as they told her Ben was fine and out of surgery," he continued. "She wanted me to leave Rocco alone."

He looked at me seriously as he spoke, "Rocco is just a puppy. I could not leave him alone in a strange house!"

"Of course not!" Gaby and I said in unison.

"Sophie, I had seen you playing with Juniper the day before. I knew where you lived." Aiden continued, "I did not know what else to do. I was sure that you would take good care of Rocco when you found him in the box."

"I'm glad you trusted me," I told him, "you did the right thing. You could not leave him home alone. He is just a puppy!"

"I lied to my Grandma. I told her I asked you if you could take care of Rocco for a few days." He said, "I guess we are in the same boat." He sighed, "I feel really bad I lied to Grandma, but I saw no other way". "You lied to Grandma?!" Ben said in disbelief. "Aiden you never lie!"
"I know Ben. Please don't tell her. I feel really bad about it."

"Everything worked out fine!" Gaby reassured us. "Stop worrying. Our parents and your grandmother don't know we lied!"

"I think we have to tell them." I mused worriedly. "I feel really bad about lying to them."
 "I agree, we have to tell them." Aiden said seriously.
"No, we can't tell them!" Gaby said, "Sophie, they will ground us for the rest of the summer!"
"Gaby, I know it will be hard, but I have to tell Dad." I said, "I just have to tell him."

Juniper was very serious.

I think Juni felt guilty also. She came over and I petted her, "Don't worry girl. It's the right thing to do." I explained to Juniper. "When you do what's right, everything always works out."

"Dad will get mad at first and he may punish me, but he will understand why I did it," I told Gaby and Aiden, "I know my Dad."

"I will tell Grandma tonight also," Aiden said. "She won't like it, but I know she will forgive me."

"Then I guess I have to tell Mom and Dad also!" Gaby was not happy, "I really don't want to tell them."

Rocco was chasing Ben up the hill. Ben was running and laughing.

I looked at them enviously and said "They are the only ones off the hook! They never lied!"

Gaby and Aiden nodded in agreement.

"I want to see the cave! Where is the cave?!!!" Ben kept demanding.

Chapter 12 – Wild Animal Tracks

"Where is the cave?" Ben asked again
Juniper barked and started running uphill.

I followed Juniper. We might as well show them the cave now, I thought. We may all be grounded by tomorrow.

"Come on Ben," I called, "I'll show you."

I froze when we got there. I could not believe we had really slept inside.
The cardboard was still in place. It was ripped in the middle. The gaping hole made a perfect door.

"It was pitch black in there last night! I was so scared!" Gaby's voice was breaking.

"This is where you slept?!" Aiden's blue eyes were transfixed as he looked at the cave. "Amazing!"

He started examining the scratch marks on the cardboard.

We told him about the sounds we heard last night when a wild animal tried to come inside.

Aiden started looking at the ground. "Look at these animal tracks" he said kneeling on the ground.

"This is awesome!" Ben screamed from inside the cave, "I love it in here!"

"Come in Rocco! Come in here Juniper!" Ben called them.

Rocco went right inside the cave. Juniper hesitated.

She finally went inside the cave but came out fast. She had her red monkey in her mouth. She loves her red monkey.

Juniper kept looking at Aiden with a worried look on her face. He was still examining the tracks on the ground.

"Juni, we are safe now," I told her as I petted her. "There is nothing to be afraid of."

Ben stuck his head out of the cave, "This cave is fantastic," he said, "I want to spend the night here tonight."

"No, you don't Ben," Gaby interrupted, "It was awful. I will never, ever, sleep in there again!"

"Neve say never," Ben continued. "Anything is possible! I don't care if it was scary, I know I will love it! Hey, there are even potato chips and peanut butter and jelly in here. Can I make myself a sandwich?"

"Sure" I answered him, "we were so scared we forgot all about the peanut butter and jelly last night."

"Make me a sandwich too," Gaby said as she crawled inside the cave with Ben.

Gaby was always hungry!

I was looking at the scratch marks on the cardboard. Juniper was standing close to me. She was still holding her red monkey in her mouth but I could feel her trembling.

Aiden kept studying the tracks on the ground. "I wonder what animal was here last night?" He asked, "there has to be a way we can figure it out" he mumbled to himself.

"Woof! Woof!" Juniper looked at me with a scared look on her face.

"I have my tablet in my book bag" He told me as he took the tablet out of the bag. "We can do a search for "wild animal tracks" and see if we can figure it out.

Juniper was still trembling next to me. I held her close, "Juni, I told you, we are safe now." I reassured her again.

Aiden sat down on the grass and started searching online. He kept swiping the screen. Every so often he would stop and look at the tracks on the ground.

"Oh no! It can't be!" Aiden exclaimed looking at the the ground and at the pictures on the tablet. "I think these are mountain lion tracks!"

Juniper walked over and stood next to Aiden. She was examining the tracks also. She barked, "Woof! Woof!"

"Sophie come here. Help me figure this out" Aiden called me. "Do you think they look like mountain lion tracks?" He asked. I sat down next to him. "Yes, they sure do!" I agreed, "a mountain lion here? That's impossible!"

Aiden was showing me the pictures on the tablet.

We had just met the day before but it felt like we had been friends forever.

I knew this was going to be an amazing summer!

The End

...to be continued in "The Mystery of the Mountain Lion Tracks" A JUST JUNIPER Adventure

ABOUT THE AUTHOR

Irene Hernández is a teacher and writer. She loves children, animals, the ocean, mountains, traveling and reading.

Her love for children, animals, and reading inspired her to write the **JUST JUNIPER Adventures.**

Irene lives in Miami, Florida where she enjoys going to the beach as often as possible!

ABOUT THE ILLUSTRATOR

Silvia María de la Fé is a talented and creative artist. She has enjoyed drawing and painting in different styles and media since her childhood.

She was encouraged by her sisters Lulú and Irene (the author) to follow her passion.

Now retired, she is enjoying drawing, painting and illustrating the **JUST JUNIPER Series!** *Silvia lives in Palm Bay, Florida with her son Joey.*

Go on more adventures with JUNIPER!

JUST JUNIPER-The First Adventure (Book 1)

The Mystery of the Mountain Lion Tracks(Book 2)

The Secret at the Lighthouse (Book 3)

Dolphins to the Rescue (Book 4)

Twin Trouble at Turtle Top (Book 5)

Coming soon...

The Disappearing Snowman (Book 6)

Dog Day at The Deering Estate (Book 7)

Barney's Big Surprise

Made in the USA
Monee, IL
11 June 2023

35604091R00059